The Hidden World

Watership Down
fiction adventures

Escape to the Hills

Rabbits in Danger

We Need More Rabbits!

Challenge to Efrafa

The Hidden World

Friend and Foe

The Hidden World

Judy Allen

RED FOX

A Red Fox Book

Published by Random House Children's Books
20 Vauxhall Bridge Road, London SW1V 2SA

A division of The Random House Group Ltd
London Melbourne Sydney Auckland
Johannesburg and agencies throughout the world

www.watershipdown.net

Illustrations by County Studio, Leicester

1 3 5 7 9 10 8 6 4 2

Printed and bound in Denmark by Nørhaven A/S

THE RANDOM HOUSE GROUP Limited Reg. No. 954009

www.randomhouse.co.uk

ISBN 0 09 940823 6

This story represents scenes from the television series, Watership Down, which is inspired by Richard Adams' novel of the same name.

Contents

The Characters of Watership Down

Hazel

The leader of the group, Hazel persuaded his friends to leave their old warren at Sandleford and start a new life elsewhere.

Fiver

One of the youngest rabbits, Hazel's brother Fiver has visions of the future – a gift that sometimes causes him many problems.

Bigwig

A former member of the Sandleford Owsla, Bigwig naturally uses force to settle any disputes and has no time for time-wasters.

Pipkin

The youngest and most vulnerable rabbit, Pipkin is innocent, sweet and adventurous, and a well-loved friend to all the group.

Blackberry

An intelligent doe, Blackberry is a great problem solver and at times of crisis, she is the calm voice of reason.

Hawkbit

Hawkbit is always ready to look on the glum side, but when the going gets tough, his loyalty to the group shines through.

Dandelion

Talker, joker and storyteller, Dandelion is always ready to celebrate the heroic deeds of the warren and El-Arah.

Kehaar

A newcomer to the group, Kehaar thinks he's much cleverer than the rabbits, but in fact he can't manage without them.

Primrose

A courageous and fearless doe, Primrose escapes from Efrafa and becomes Hazel's partner and mother of his children.

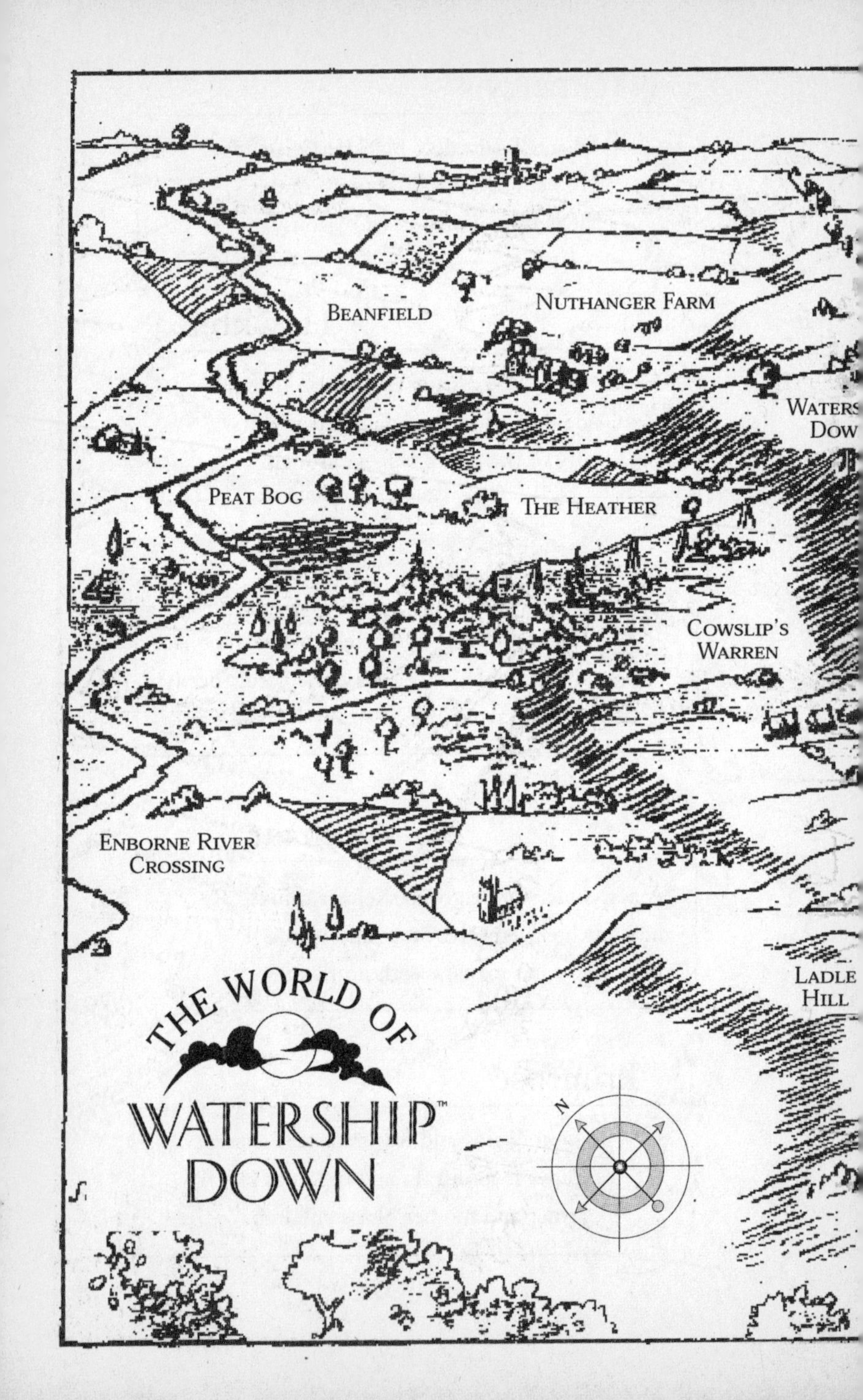

BEANFIELD
NUTHANGER FARM
PEAT BOG
THE HEATHER
COWSLIP'S
WARREN
ENBORNE RIVER
CROSSING
LADLE
HILL
THE WORLD OF
WATERSHIP™
DOWN
N

Mansion
Upper Bridge
Efrafa
Lower Bridge
Railway Arch
Railway Crossing
Whitchurch

CHAPTER ONE

Homesick

For once there was no work to be done in the warren on Watership Down. Most of the rabbits lay on the grass outside, enjoying the sunshine. Only Primrose sat alone, looking out over the edge of the down.

After a while, Hazel and Fiver

hopped over to her.

'Are you all right?' said Hazel.

Primrose sighed. 'I've been thinking about my home warren, Redstone,' she said. 'I haven't seen it since I was captured and taken to Efrafa. All the time I was a prisoner, I dreamt of home. Hazel, I want to go back to Redstone.'

'I hoped you were happy here,' said Hazel.

'I am,' said Primrose. 'This place is everything a rabbit could ask for... but... I'm homesick.'

Fiver shivered and closed his eyes. 'Redstone warren is empty and dead,' he whispered. 'It only lives inside your head.'

'What is he talking about?' said Primrose, startled.

'Fiver has visions,' said Hazel, looking anxiously at his younger brother.

'His vision is wrong!' said Primrose. 'Redstone's still there – it has to be.' She turned and ran back to the warren.

Fiver shook himself awake. 'I'm sorry,' he said miserably.

'It's not your fault,' said Hazel.

'Maybe I am wrong,' said Fiver, hopefully. 'Maybe Redstone is still there.'

'There's only one way to find out,' said Hazel.

Next day he woke Primrose early, and together they set out to find her old home. At first their journey was easy, along the slopes of the downs and through meadows full of wild flowers. But then they came to a canal.

Hazel checked the towpath in both directions. 'I can't see any way across,' he said.

'But Redstone's on the other side,' said Primrose. 'Just beyond those woods.'

A steady clomping sound drew closer, and a large horse appeared round a bend in the path, towing a barge. The rabbits dodged out of sight until the horse had gone by. When they crept out again, the barge was moving past in front of them.

'Here's how we cross!' said Primrose. Bravely she jumped onto the barge and ran across it.

'Be careful!' shouted Hazel – but he had to follow.

Together, they leapt from the barge towards the opposite bank of the canal.

Hazel landed safely, but Primrose fell in. The barge moved on, leaving her scrabbling desperately at the wall of the canal.

'I can't climb out,' she cried, struggling and swimming.

Hazel ran along the canal bank

above her. 'Keep going,' he called. 'We'll find a way out.'

'I can't...' gasped Primrose.

'You can!' shouted Hazel. 'You must!'

The sound of an engine startled them. A houseboat was chugging along the canal towards Primrose. It passed without touching her, but the fright was too much. She began to sink.

At once Hazel dived in. He caught the scruff of her neck with his teeth, held her head above water and swam with her along the canal.

Soon they came to a lock. Hazel pulled Primrose through the huge gates just as they were closing.

The houseboat was already in the lock, its engine quiet. Hazel towed Primrose along its side. The water level was sinking, but it was still very deep.

The gates on the far side of the lock opened. The houseboat's engine roared into life and it moved out at full speed. The wake caught Hazel and Primrose, tumbling them over and over. Within seconds they had disappeared, dragged down by the churning white water.

CHAPTER TWO

The Spirits of Redstone

Hazel and Primrose bobbed to the surface in quiet water below the lock gate. They had been swept out of the canal into a peaceful stretch of river. They managed to struggle to the sloping bank and climb out. There they collapsed, exhausted.

The hooting of an owl woke Hazel. He sat up, surprised to find that night had fallen and the moon was shining. Gently, he shook Primrose awake.

Primrose sat up. 'You jumped into the water to save me – even though you knew we might both be drowned,' she said.

'I love you,' said Hazel simply. Then he stood up, embarrassed, and headed for the woods. 'Come on,' he said. 'We can't stay here. The owls are hunting.'

For a while they hopped together through the trees. Then Primrose raced ahead and scampered down into a hollow, calling, 'This is it, Hazel! This is Redstone! Home...'

She stopped. Redstone warren was still and silent. The burrows were crumbling, their entrances overgrown with ivy and weeds.

'Poppy?' called Primrose, looking around. 'Lavender? Anyone?'

Hazel sniffed the air. 'The scent is old,' he said. 'This warren was abandoned a long time ago.'

'Fiver was right,' said Primrose, her ears drooping. 'Redstone warren is empty and dead.'

A sudden shout startled them. An old grey rabbit had appeared out of a burrow at the far end of the warren. 'Who goes there?' he called.

'Captain Broom!' said Primrose.

'Primrose?' said the old grey rabbit. 'Primrose! You've come back!'

'What happened here?' said Primrose.

Captain Broom sighed. 'A terrible sickness,' he said. 'The Black Rabbit of Inle took everyone. Everyone but me.'

Then he brightened. 'Oh look,' he said, 'there's Lavender.'

Hazel and Primrose looked where he pointed – but there was no one there.

'Lavender,' said Captain Broom, hobbling a little way off and talking to the empty air, 'come and greet Primrose. You too, Sage – and the rest of you.'

'Poor Captain Broom,' said Primrose softly.

Hazel shook his head, his eyes sad.

'Every night, in my dreams,' said Primrose, 'I'd leave Efrafa and come home and everyone was here. But they weren't really here. They'd gone with the Black Rabbit of Inle.'

'They were still here in a way,' said Hazel. 'Their spirits stayed because you needed them while you were a prisoner. Now it's time to set them free.'

Primrose nodded, her eyes bright with tears. 'I'll never forget them,' she said, 'but now I know the truth, I can let them go.'

'Don't cry,' said Hazel. 'You have me, and you have Watership Down.'

Captain Broom hopped over to them. He looked puzzled. 'Lavender just said goodbye,' he said. 'Then the others said goodbye, too, and now they've all gone. I don't understand.'

Hazel touched his shoulder. 'We're taking you home with us, Captain Broom,' he said. 'To a place in the high hills.'

'The most beautiful place in the world,' said Primrose.

'Sounds lovely,' said Captain Broom, 'and I suppose I can't stay here alone.'

Gently, the two young rabbits led him away from the deserted warren.

At the top of the slope Primrose turned back. 'Goodbye, everyone,' she whispered, 'and thank you.'

They travelled back slowly, using the top of the lock gates as a bridge to cross the canal, and reached Watership Down at dawn.

Almost all the rabbits popped out of the warren to greet them. Only Hawkbit was missing. When at last he appeared, he looked scared and dusty.

'Hawkbit!' said Dandelion. 'You look as if you've seen the Black Rabbit of Inle!'

Blackberry looked up, startled.

'Did you really see him, Hawkbit?' said Pipkin.

'Of course not!' said Hawkbit. But his eyes were frightened.

'Settle down, everyone,' said Bigwig firmly. 'Forget the Black Rabbit. We have a new friend to welcome.' As the others crowded around Captain Broom, Hazel took Hawkbit aside.

'What happened?' he asked quietly.

'I discovered something in the warren,' Hawkbit whispered. 'Something really strange.'

CHAPTER THREE

Deep Danger

'Hawkbit,' said Hazel, 'I think you'd better show me your strange discovery.'

Hawkbit led Hazel into the warren.

'Something tells me we should be careful,' said Fiver, following them reluctantly.

As the three rabbits hopped through the main burrow, a rumbling sound came from far below. It echoed around the warren and died away.

'I don't like the sound of that,' said Fiver.

'It's what I heard before,' said Hawkbit. 'It came from here.' He led the way to an abandoned burrow, scattered with earth and rubble.

The rumbling came again, louder. A chilly draught ruffled the rabbits' fur and a weird, pale light shone up from the floor.

'Blackberry warned us to stay out of this section,' said Fiver. 'She thought the floor might collapse.'

'She could be right,' said Hawkbit. He pointed to a narrow opening in the floor ahead. He and Hazel crept forward and looked down it. Phosphorescent light shone up from it, throwing their shadows against the tunnel walls.

The rumbling came again. The burrow floor shook – and a moment later it split open. Hazel and Hawkbit dropped headlong into the chasm.

As Fiver looked wildly around for something to

hold onto, the floor tilted and tipped him in after them. Earth, rubble and pieces of dead tree root cascaded in behind him. Everything was darkness and dust. Then the dust settled, and the rabbits scrambled to their feet and looked around.

They were in an enormous chamber with many tunnels leading out of it. Pointed stalagmites grew up from the floor. Twisted stalactites hung from the roof. The walls glowed with eerie light.

'We've fallen into a cavern below our warren,' said Hazel.

'I don't think there's any way back up,' said Hawkbit.

Hazel looked at the pile of rubble that had tumbled down after them. 'If we try to dig through that,' he said, 'it'll fall in on top of us. We'd better wait till the others dig us out from above.'

'But they won't know where we are!' said Hawkbit.

'It's cold and damp and the ceiling's dripping,' said Fiver. 'Maybe we should look for another way out.'

'All right,' said Hazel. 'I smell fresh air. There must be an opening somewhere.'

'But which way?' said Fiver. 'There are tunnels in every direction.'

'It doesn't matter,' said Hawkbit impatiently. 'Let's just get moving.'

'We'll try this tunnel here,' said Hazel, calmly.

The tunnel grew even narrower as they moved through it, but the smell of fresh air drew them on.

Suddenly Fiver stopped – gripped by a vision. 'A black space below – swallows any who go,' he murmured. He shook himself and called, 'Hazel! Look out!'

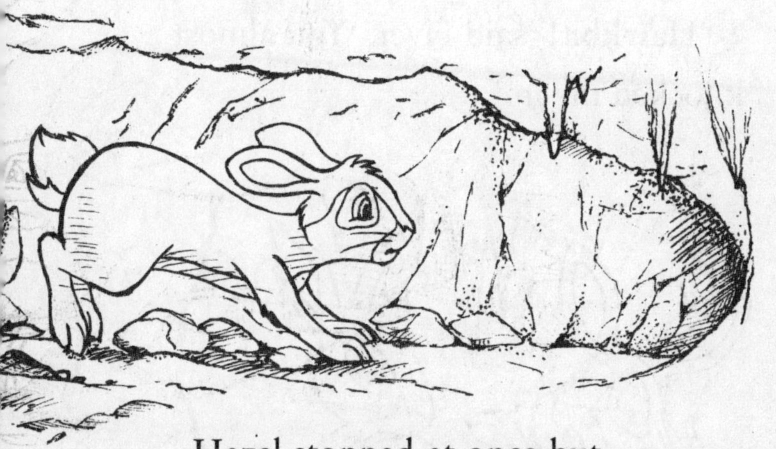

Hazel stopped at once but Hawkbit was desperate to keep going. He pushed between Hazel and Fiver, sending Fiver staggering towards a hole that dropped down into nothingness.

Hazel grabbed Fiver and pulled him to safety. Loose stones rattled into the pit, their sound fading to silence before they touched the bottom.

'Hawkbit!' said Fiver. 'You almost knocked me in.'

'You said there was fresh air this way!' said Hawkbit, his eyes wide. 'I have to get out!' He turned and ran, back the way they had come.

'Quick, Fiver,' said Hazel. 'We must catch him. He's in a blind panic. We mustn't let him get lost.'

CHAPTER FOUR

The Search Party

It wasn't long before the others noticed that Hazel, Fiver and Hawkbit were missing. Bigwig immediately organised a search of the hillside and the warren, but no one could find any sign of the lost rabbits.

'Three missing!' said Dandelion.

'The Black Rabbit of Inle must have taken them!'

'No need for talk like that,' said Bigwig, briskly. 'We must search the deepest burrows.'

Blackberry, Primrose and the rest set off immediately, but Dandelion and Pipkin hung back.

'I don't want to go into the deepest burrows if the Black Rabbit's down there,' said Dandelion.

'Neither do I,' squeaked Pipkin.

'I know you're afraid,' said Bigwig, gently. 'But remember,

fear makes you alert and aware. Fear can make you stronger.'

'It can?' said Dandelion.

'Definitely!' said Bigwig.

'Can we go together?' said Pipkin.

'YES!' said Bigwig, losing patience. 'But hop to it!'

By the time Pipkin and Dandelion got going, every deep burrow but one was already being searched. Only the abandoned burrow was left.

Cautiously they crept in. 'Remember,' whispered Dandelion. 'Fear makes you strong.'

'I'm so frightened, I must be as strong as a tree,' said Pipkin, his voice quavering.

They crept on until they came to the hole in the floor. Even though it was blocked with rubble, a faint eerie light shone up from it. It threw the shadow of an enormous rabbit onto the burrow wall.

'The Black Rabbit of Inle!' screamed Dandelion.

His yell brought the others running from all directions.

'It's your own shadow!' said Blackberry. 'Look, there's mine, next to it.'

Dandelion hung his head. 'That's the trouble with being a Keeper of Stories,' he mumbled. 'My imagination gets out of hand.'

'I wonder,' said Blackberry, looking at the rubble-filled hole. 'Could Hazel and the others possibly be down there?'

At that moment, Kehaar the gull landed at the main entrance to the warren. His loud squawking sounded throughout the burrows. 'Beegveeg!' he called. 'Come quick. I see Efrafa patrol! Led by Campion and Vervain.'

'Where?' said Bigwig, hurrying out to him.

'Pretty close,' said Kehaar.

'Maybe Hazel and the others aren't down the hole,' said Bigwig. 'Maybe they've been caught by the Efrafans.'

He paused just long enough to shout to Blackberry, 'Keep everyone searching. I'm going on solitary patrol.' Then he turned to Kehaar, his face grim. 'Lead me to them,' he said.

But even from above, Kehaar couldn't see the Efrafans any more. 'Too much trees,' he said. 'Too much bushes. Bunnies out of sight.'

'They'll be heading for Efrafa,' said Bigwig, 'so that's where we'll go too.' And he began to run.

He was a big strong rabbit and he moved so fast that even Kehaar was impressed.

When he reached the stone bridge close to Woundwort's warren, two guards stepped forward at once.

'I recognise you!' said the first guard. 'You betrayed Efrafa, insulted our general and stole two of our rabbits. We're taking you prisoner.'

'Come on then,' said Bigwig. 'Try it.'

As the two guards rushed at him, Bigwig charged. He slammed into the pair of them, knocking them flat. Within seconds he had his sharp foreclaws at their throats. 'Has the patrol brought back prisoners?' he demanded.

'No,' said both guards, their voices squeaky with fright.

'You wouldn't lie to me, would you?' said Bigwig.

'No,' said the first guard shakily. 'Owsla's honour.'

Bigwig released the guards and stepped back. 'Much good you are,' he said scornfully.

But at that moment, Campion and Vervain appeared beside the bridge, followed by the rest of the patrol.

'Time to go!' said Bigwig, and he turned and bolted to the river's edge.

'Get him!' yelled Vervain, heading the chase.

Bigwig raced along the river bank, leaping over rocks and crashing through reeds. Behind him, Kehaar swooped low, flying into Vervain and knocking him off his feet.

Bigwig just had time to crouch behind a fallen log, near a weeping willow, then Vervain was up again, leading the patrol in a furious charge.

'He hasn't crossed the river,' yelled Vervain triumphantly, 'He must be close by. Patrol – move in!'

CHAPTER FIVE

The World Below

In the hidden world below Watership Down, Hawkbit ran. He ran till he came to a cave where crystal sheets hung from the ceiling, shiny as mirrors. His own reflection, repeated a thousand times, came racing towards him. Thinking he was being attacked by a mob of rabbits,

Hawkbit screamed, slipped, and fell into the crystal sheets, making them shatter.

He wasn't hurt, but he was terrified. Hazel and Fiver found him huddled on the floor. 'We'll never get out,' he sobbed.

Fiver sat down beside him. 'Listen,' he said. 'We found Watership Down because we believed we would. And we'll get out of here if we believe we can.'

'It's easy for you,' Hawkbit whimpered. 'You're not afraid.'

'Yes I am,' said Fiver. He leant closer and whispered, 'So is Hazel. It's all right to be afraid. What you mustn't do is give up hope.'

'Oh,' said Hawkbit, feeling a bit calmer.

'Let's get going,' said Hazel.

Hawkbit nodded and got to his feet.

They left the crystal cave and moved on through the dark tunnels. Soon they heard running water, and all at once they found themselves on a narrow ledge at the top of a deep cave. Carefully, they followed the ledge as it wound its way down to a stream running across the cave floor.

Hazel looked along it. 'I see daylight,' he said. 'I'll check if it's safe.'

'No, I will,' said Hawkbit. 'You got us this far. It's my turn to be brave.'

He waded through the stream to the cave-mouth. It was covered by the fronds of a weeping willow.

Pushing them aside he saw something amazing – Bigwig hiding behind a log, with Vervain and Campion closing in on him.

'Bigwig,' hissed Hawkbit.

Bigwig blinked in surprise. Then he darted through the willow fronds and followed Hawkbit back to the cave.

The Watership Down rabbits listened as the Efrafan patrol searched outside.

Soon Campion called out, 'We've lost him,' and Vervain shouted back, 'Search the riverbank. He must have gone upstream.'

As the sound of the Efrafans faded away, Bigwig said, 'How in Frith's name did you get here?'

'We'll tell you on the way home,' said Hazel.

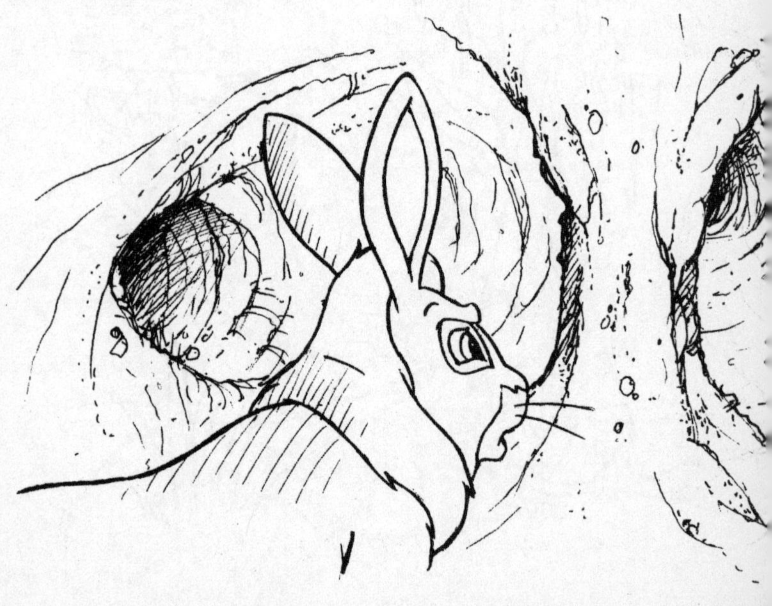

They walked back to Watership Down overground, but when they arrived the warren was deserted.

'I know we've been away a while,' said Bigwig, 'but how can everyone have disappeared?'

When they'd searched everywhere else, they walked cautiously into the abandoned burrow.

The hole they had fallen down was enormous now and there, at the bottom of a newly dug rabbit-run, were all the others, even Captain Broom.

'Hazel!' said Primrose, looking up. 'You're safe!'

'What are you doing up there?' said Dandelion. 'We came down here to rescue you.'

Hazel, Fiver, Bigwig and Hawkbit joined them in the great cavern with its luminous walls and sparkling stalactites.

'Once we were terrified down here,' said Fiver. 'Now it feels safe – and beautiful.'

‘And we’ve found a secret way to the edge of Efrafa,’ said Bigwig.

‘AND,’ said Hazel, standing close beside Primrose, ‘I’ve got some news – I’m going to be a father.’

At once the cavern was filled with the sound of everyone cheering and shouting, ‘Baby rabbits! Baby rabbits for Watership Down!’

Glossary

OF ESSENTIAL RABBIT WORDS

Buck	A male rabbit
Doe	A female rabbit
Efrafa	The name of General Woundwort's warren
El-Arah	The shortened name of the rabbit hero, El-ahrairah. The many stories of El-Arah are an inspiration to all rabbits
Elil	Enemies of rabbits; like foxes, hawks and weasels
Flayrah	Good food; like carrots, cabbages and lettuces
Frith	The sun; a god to the rabbits

Frithmas	The rabbits' Christmas celebration; it is celebrated with a great feast
Inle	The moon; when it is time for a rabbit to die, the Black Rabbit of Inle comes to fetch him
Owsla	A group of strong brave rabbits who are trained to defend the warren
Silflay	Eating outside the warren; usually at dawn or dusk
Warren	The network of burrows where rabbits live

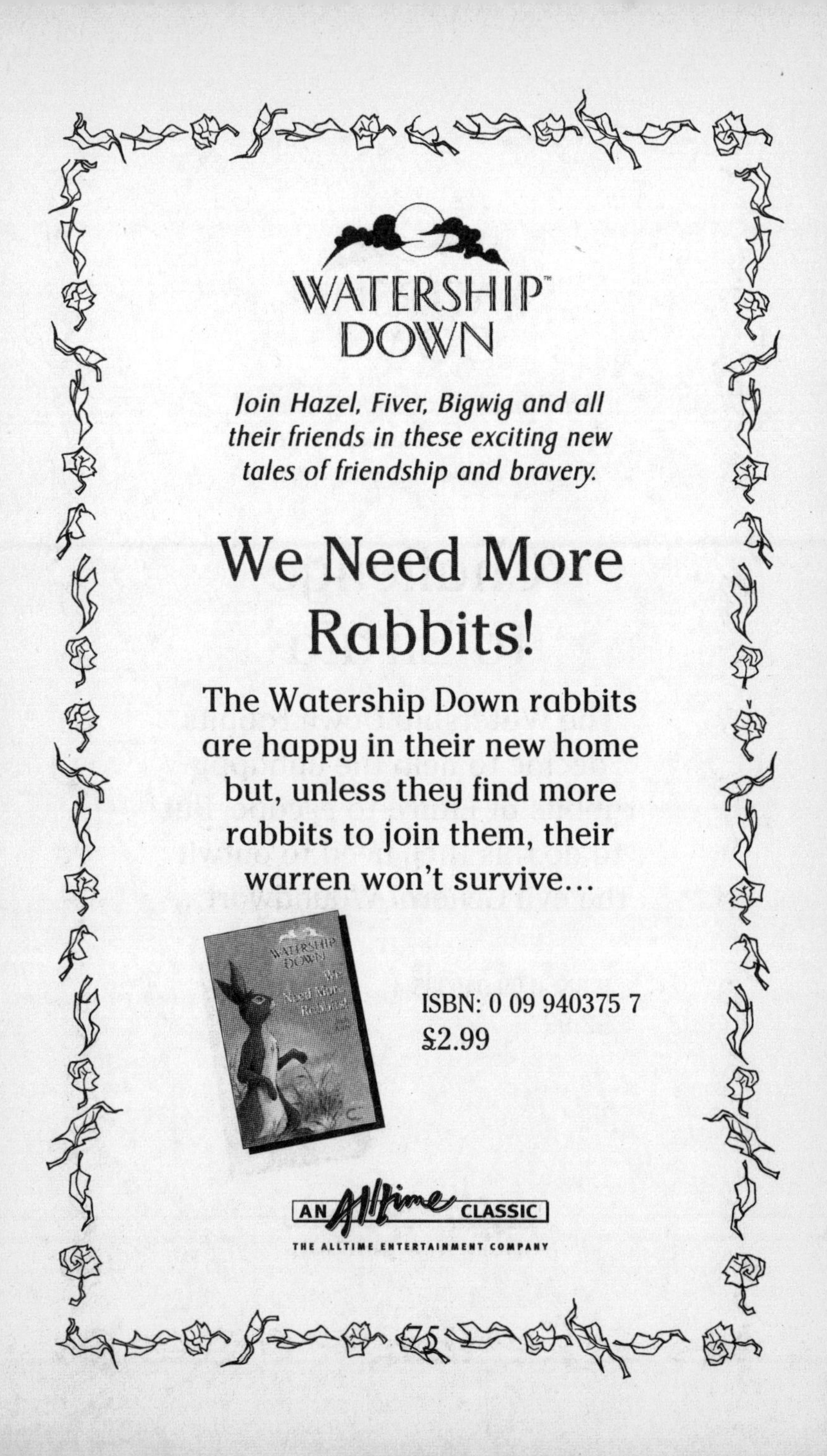
WATERSHIP DOWN
Join Hazel, Fiver, Bigwig and all their friends in these exciting new tales of friendship and bravery.
We Need More Rabbits!
The Watership Down rabbits are happy in their new home but, unless they find more rabbits to join them, their warren won't survive...
ISBN: 0 09 940375 7
£2.99
AN Alltime CLASSIC
THE ALLTIME ENTERTAINMENT COMPANY

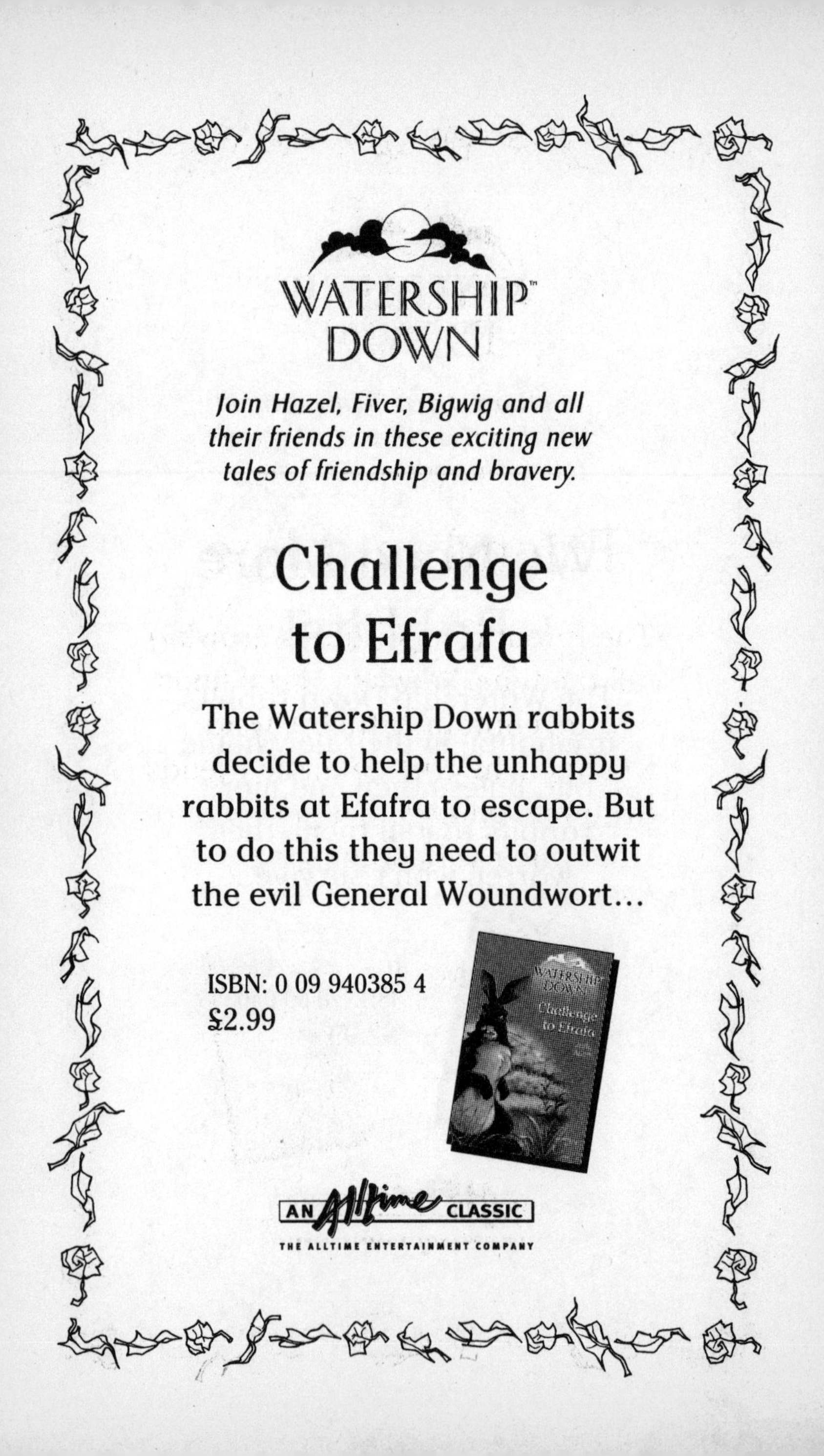
WATERSHIP™
DOWN
Join Hazel, Fiver, Bigwig and all
their friends in these exciting new
tales of friendship and bravery.
Challenge
to Efrafa
The Watership Down rabbits
decide to help the unhappy
rabbits at Efafra to escape. But
to do this they need to outwit
the evil General Woundwort...
ISBN: 0 09 940385 4
£2.99
AN Alltime CLASSIC
THE ALLTIME ENTERTAINMENT COMPANY

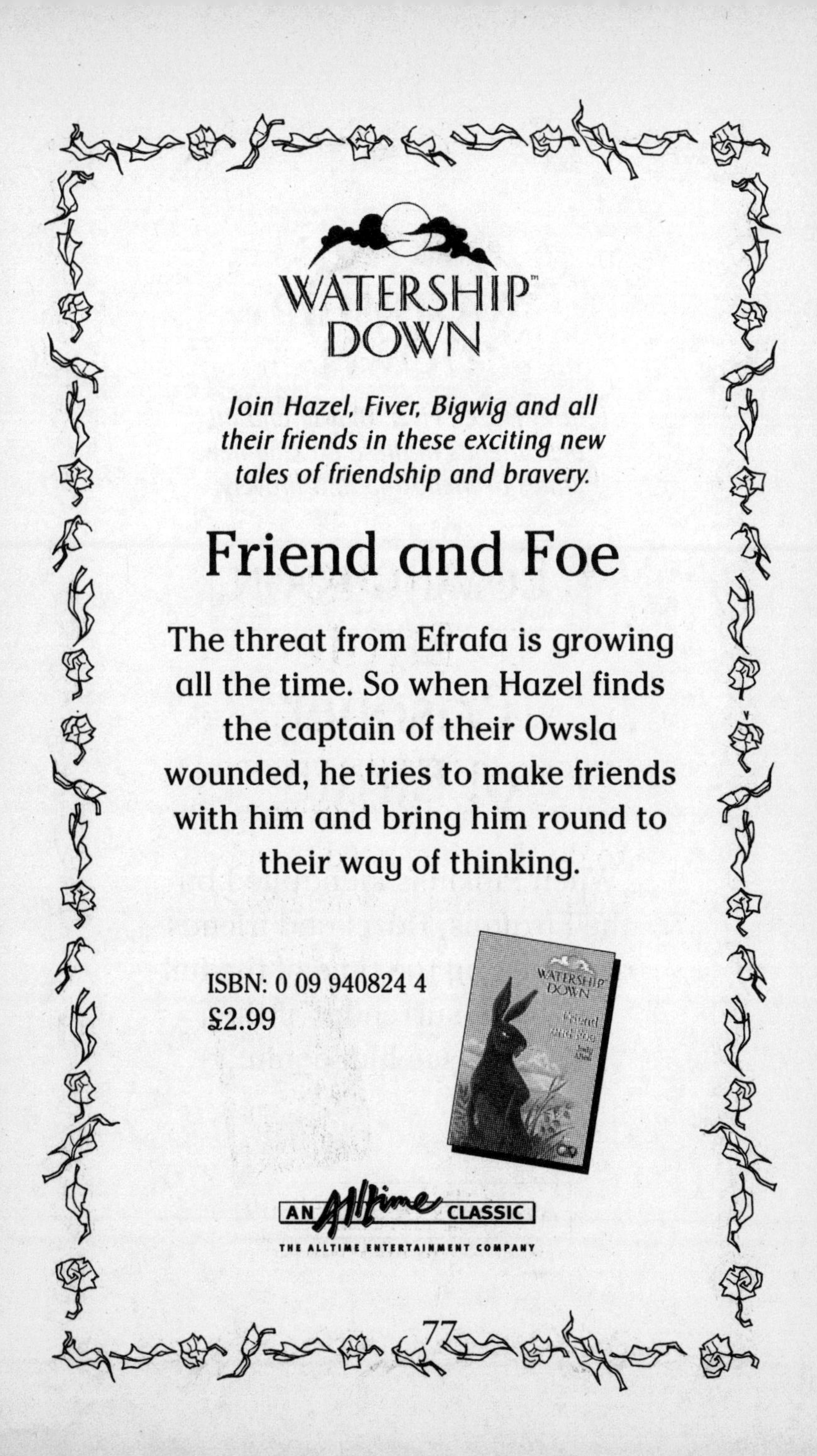
WATERSHIP™
DOWN
Join Hazel, Fiver, Bigwig and all
their friends in these exciting new
tales of friendship and bravery.
Friend and Foe
The threat from Efrafa is growing
all the time. So when Hazel finds
the captain of their Owsla
wounded, he tries to make friends
with him and bring him round to
their way of thinking.
ISBN: 0 09 940824 4
£2.99
WATERSHIP
DOWN
AN Alltime CLASSIC
THE ALLTIME ENTERTAINMENT COMPANY

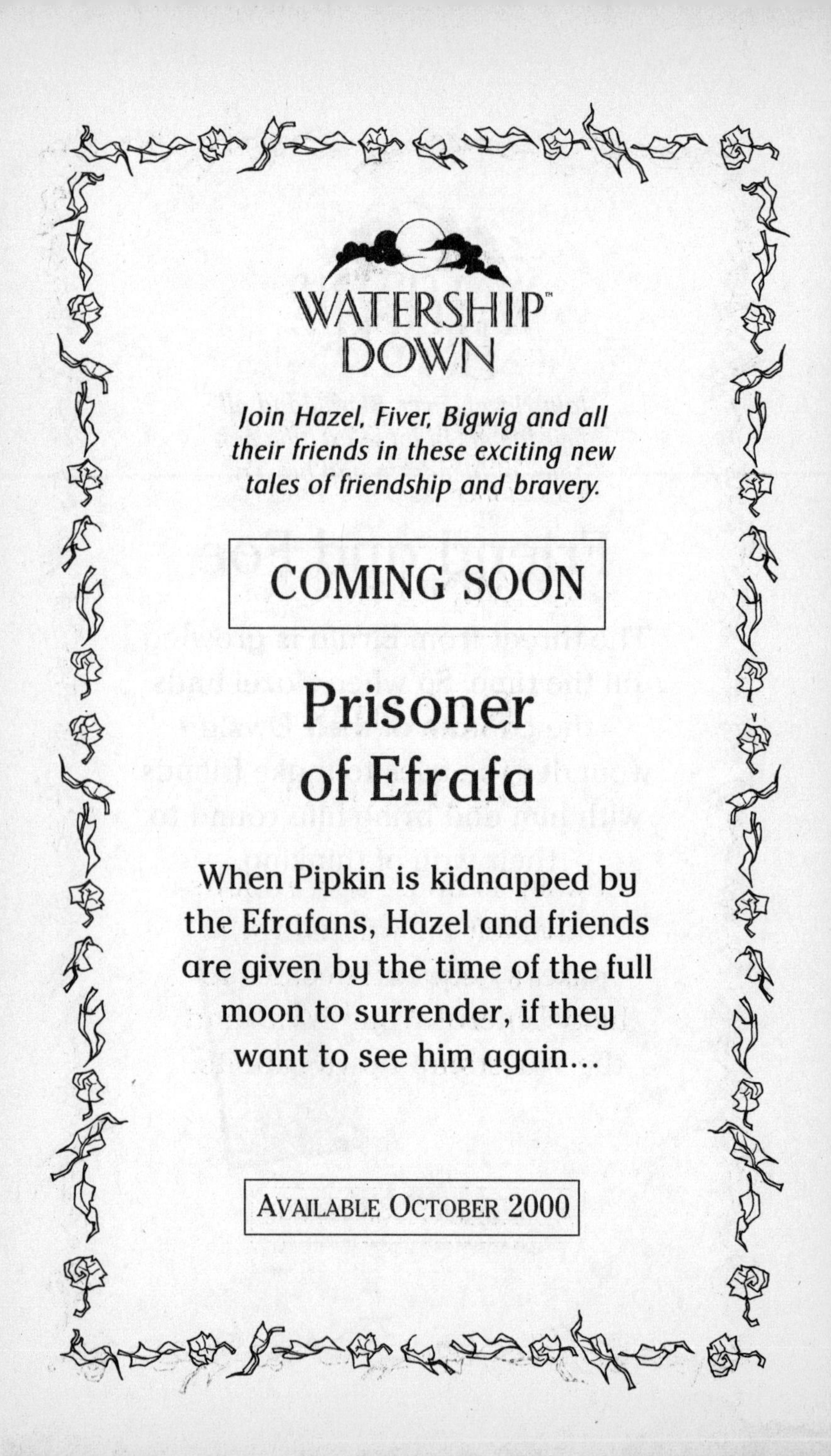

WATERSHIP™
DOWN
Join Hazel, Fiver, Bigwig and all
their friends in these exciting new
tales of friendship and bravery.
COMING SOON
Prisoner
of Efrafa
When Pipkin is kidnapped by
the Efrafans, Hazel and friends
are given by the time of the full
moon to surrender, if they
want to see him again...
AVAILABLE OCTOBER 2000

WATERSHIP DOWN
Join Hazel, Fiver, Bigwig and all their friends in these exciting new tales of friendship and bravery.
COMING SOON
Rabbits Betrayed
Cowslip is angry that rabbits have left his warren with Hazel's help and decides to help General Woundwort find the Watership Down rabbits.
AVAILABLE OCTOBER 2000